Mail Order Bride:
The Bride's Mysterious
Husband

By
Faith Johnson

Clean and Wholesome Western
Historical Romance

Table of Contents

Unsolicited Testimonials

By **Glaidene Ramsey**
★★★★★ I so enjoy reading Faith Johnson's stories. This Bride and groom met as she arrived in town. They were married and then the story begins.!!!! Enjoy

By **Voracious Reader**
★★★★★ "Great story of love and of faith. The hardships we may have to go through and how with faith, and God's help we can get through them" -

By **Glaidene's reads**
★★★★★ "Faith Johnson is a five star writer. I have read a majority of her books. I enjoyed the story and hope you will too!!!!!"

By **Kirk Statler**
★★★★★ I liked the book. A different twist because she wasn't in contract with anyone when she went. She went. God provided for her needs. God blessed her above and beyond.

By **Amazon Customer**
★★★★★ Great clean and easy reading, a lot of fun for you to know ignores words this is crazy so I'll not reviewing again. Let me tell it and go

By **Kindle Customer**
★★★★★ Wonderful story. You have such a way of showing people that opposite do attack. Both in words and action. I am glad that I found your books.

Chapter 1

"I cannot believe that you published that advertisement without my permission, mother!"

"You wouldn't have allowed me to do it either way," Ann Rhodes replied to her daughter.

Cassie had never felt so angry in her life. Moreover, she had never raised her voice at her own mother before. During her early childhood, Cassie had always been told to act like a lady. Act like a lady, and you shall marry well.

She followed that rule until the age of twenty. Today, she broke that rule.

Cassie did everything in her power to stay composed, but her mother's actions pushed her over the edge. She had never experienced a betrayal so grand.

"This is barbaric," Cassie said, bending over to push her clothing into a tattered suitcase.

It was clear that she was never going to win an argument in this household. There was no point in retaliating. Cassie knew her new fate as soon as her mother placed that letter on the desk. Therefore, she decided to start packing her belongings before anybody could tell her to do so. She wanted to maintain some kind of power.

"It isn't barbaric, Cassandra," Ann replied. "This is our only way out."

Cassie bit her tongue. Her words weren't enough to change anything anyway.

"We are very close to losing the house." Ann looked down at her folded hands as she stood by her daughter's bed. "Maybe things would have been different if your father was still here. But we cannot survive on our own. We simply do not have the money."

"Maybe we would have more money if you allowed me to publish those poems."

Ann rolled her eyes, turning her gaze to the window. "Please, don't start this again."

It was almost as if Cassie had grown immune to her mother's doubts about her passion. Cassie had been writing ever since she was six. It was the only skill that she was proud to have mastered. But her mother thought that it was a waste of time.

There was no point in trying to convince her otherwise. Ann Rhodes was a skeptic.

Cassie shook her head as she closed the suitcase with both hands. When she looked down at them, she could see her fingers trembling.

Anger was her initial emotion. But deep down, she was afraid.

Cassie was about to travel to California. She was about to marry a stranger. Everything that she had known before would be tossed out with the garbage. She was starting her life from scratch.

After a few seconds, Cassie felt her mother's hand on her shoulder. It was gentle, but firm.

"Look at me, Cassandra."

Cassie bit the inside of her cheek as she straightened up and turned on her heels. Her mother was looking down at her with her chin pointed upwards.

Despite their economic struggles, Ann Rhodes always presented herself as a woman of means. Perhaps her forceful personality did most of the work.

Cassie clenched her fists and raised both shoulders as Ann moved her hand to cradle her cheek. Any other time, Cassie would have leaned into her touch. But on this day, her palm felt cold. Alien.

"You know that I love you," Ann said calmly. "That is why I am doing this. You might be angry with me right now, but in the future... you will thank me. You'll learn all about the sacrifices that I have made to keep you off the streets."

Cassie couldn't look her in the eye. How could she possibly sympathize with her?

"You have to keep the letter." Ann glanced over to the folded paper on the desk as she lowered her hand. "It has the address and any other information you need for the journey. As well as that, your future husband was kind enough to provide you with the money you will need for the train fare. Isn't that something?"

Cassie couldn't tell whether her mother was actually getting swooned by a stranger. It was as if his contribution was enough to speak for him as a person.

"Write to me as soon as you get to California." Ann took a step back, casting a hopeful glance towards the suitcase on the bed. "I will be expecting a letter."

Cassie waited for her mother to leave her room before she allowed herself to burst into tears.

She ran to the window and pressed her head against the brick wall beside her. The vision of North Carolina began to get blurry in her eyes. She felt her stomach dropping. She couldn't help but feel like a prized cow that was getting shipped across the country to end up cornered in a dark slaughterhouse.

Her life was ending. She was going to become a shell of a person.

Cassie sniffled, wiping her eyes with the sleeve of her dress. She turned to look at the letter that was still on her desk. She wished that she could make it burn.

After a few minutes, Cassie finally found the courage to walk up to it. With a sigh, she picked up the letter, watching as a few dollar bills scattered to the floor. She didn't bother to pick them up. She was more interested in the words on the page.

Cassie unfolded the paper in her hands and scanned through the handwritten text. Her mind decided to ignore most of it. It was only when she got to the bottom of the letter that her attention was grabbed again.

It had been signed.

John Walker.

***

Cassie felt her heart hammering against her chest when she stepped off the train. The California weather was stuffy, and she could barely catch her breath. She wasn't used to such heat.

Stepping forward, Cassie grabbed the tip of her hat and pulled it down. She was aware of all the people on the platform, and it made her nervous to think that one of them could be her future husband. She wasn't ready.

What was she doing?

She wasn't ready at all.

"Here's your luggage, miss." A train worker rolled her suitcase closer to her feet.

Cassie mumbled a thank you, barely able to hear her own voice. She was very faint. Her mouth was dry. She wanted to go home.

The train whistled behind her as she clutched John's letter to her chest. She placed her hand on the handle of the suitcase in order to look occupied. It was just a matter of time before somebody would feel brave enough to approach her.

There was a lot of chatter on the train platform. Most of the voices belonged to men.

She heard the train screeching behind her as it started to roll away. Her hat was still obstructing her view. She didn't want anybody to see her face. She was embarrassed to be here.

A few minutes later, Cassie saw a pair of brown boots appearing in her peripheral vision. They stopped two feet away from her.

Her shoulders tensed up. She knew exactly who the boots belonged to.

"Miss Rhodes?"

Cassie swallowed the lump in her throat before peeking out from underneath her hat. Her gaze fell on a burly man wearing a rancher's clothes. After their eyes met, it took less than two seconds for him to look away.

That must have been John.

"There you are," he said, glancing over to her suitcase. "I've been waiting for a while."

Without any further hesitation, John picked up Cassie's suitcase as if it weighed nothing. For a brief moment, she wondered how he was able to recognize her. But when she glanced around, it was evident that her dress stood out from the rest. It appeared as though Californian women were more practical with their fashion. Cassie wore her dress as if she were ready to step out onto a stage.

"We are to be married within the hour," he said. "I assume that you have no objections to that."

Cassie blinked at him, finally finding her voice. "Excuse me?"

John sighed, fighting every opportunity to look her in the eyes.

"The preacher is in town," he said. "The sooner that we are married, the better. I have other matters to attend to."

Cassie felt her cheeks flushing.

"My name is John, by the way," he added reluctantly. "John Walker."

Her life didn't feel real. Cassie was under the impression that if a man was so set on marrying her, he'd at least have the courtesy to be more polite.

But John acted as if this was just a business deal. And perhaps it was, for both of their families.

***

John didn't talk much, she learned quickly. It was like he couldn't think of anything to say. It was clear that his heart wasn't in this ordeal. Something troubled him.

Cassie glanced down at the ring on her finger. She felt like she had blinked and then traveled forward in time. She had memories of the wedding, if she could even call it that, but she didn't remember being present. The preacher's voice was a monologue echoing in her head. Cassie only had to utter two words during the ceremony that took place in a small room. That was how easy it was to sign her life away.

"I got us a wagon," John spoke up, catching her by surprise.

Indeed, when they stopped walking, a wagon was in front of them. Cassie swallowed hard.

"It will take us to the ranch," he said. "That's where I live."

Cassie was about to reply when John stepped forward and opened the door to the vehicle. The driver smiled down at the new couple, greeting them with a nod.

John cleared his throat, gesturing to the wagon. "Miss."

"Oh... thank you," she muttered back.

Cassie grabbed his hand as he helped her into the wagon. Once she sat down, she could hear John throwing her suitcase into the back. The whole wagon shook.

Quickly, she glanced down at her hand again.

She was married. And she belonged to a stranger.

John climbed in beside her and shut the door of the wagon. Cassie feared that she would have suffocated in such a small space if it wasn't for the opened windows.

When the wagon began to move, Cassie glanced out onto the street. The dusty road made it hard to see the people walking by. It was as if the California haze tried to blind her.

Cassie sat back and directed her gaze to her new husband.

John had both of his hands on his knees. He was tapping one foot against the ground. She had never had so much trouble with reading a person before. Was he anxious? Was he worried? Did he feel the same emotions that she felt?

Or did he not care about the whole thing at all?

She tried to place herself in his shoes. John had spent a lot of money to get her to this state. On top of that, he had rented a wagon when they could have easily ridden a horse back to his ranch.

Maybe he wasn't stone-cold, but it was too early to tell. At least her new husband was handsome. His short stubble suggested that he had lived through a stressful week, but it suited him. He was handsome without trying to be, unlike all the men back in North Carolina.

"Is it a long ride?" Cassie asked timidly.

John took a while to reply. It made Cassie feel like he was trying to ignore her.

"Twenty minutes," he said.

It was evident that there was no backing out now. The least she could do was learn how to tolerate it.

Chapter 2

When the wagon was pulled to a stop, Cassie almost went flying off her seat.

"We're here!" the driver called out from the front.

John sighed deeply before climbing out of the wagon. For a second, Cassie was convinced that he wasn't going to help her out. Why would he? Yes, she was now his wife... but what did that change in the grand scheme of things?

They were barely acquainted.

And so Cassie was pleasantly surprised when John opened her side of the door and offered her his hand. She took it.

When she stepped onto the dusty ground, Cassie realized that John was still avoiding as much eye contact as he could.

"Thank you," she said.

John nodded curtly before walking over to the back of the wagon.

Was there a point in trying? Cassie couldn't help but wonder what her mother would have thought about all of this. Would she be happy for her? Or would she have concerns?

Cassie placed a hand over her forehead to shade her eyes from the sun. She tried to steady her breathing as she stared ahead at the ranch house. There were no other buildings in sight. This must be her home.

It was a modest building on a vast plot of land. When Cassie shifted her eyes to the left, she could see a few corrals amongst the reddish dust. Two horses were pulling dry hay out of a hay rack that had been nailed to a fence. Cassie couldn't see any other animals, but then she noticed a red barn on the other side of the ranch. The others must have been inside.

She had no idea what it took to maintain a ranch, but perhaps John did not have enough time to care for everything. Maybe that was why he paid for her arrival.

Cassie looked back at her new husband, who was already carrying her suitcase toward the house's porch. She glanced back at the driver quickly and shot him a polite smile.

"Thank you for the ride, mister," she said.

The driver smiled back at her. Within a few seconds, the wagon was rolling in the direction of the nearest town, leaving nothing but a cloud of dust behind it.

When Cassie looked back at John, he was opening the front door of the ranch house. Without further hesitation, she rushed over to his side, ignoring the dull headache that was coming with the heat of the sun.

The house was even hotter than the outside. It took Cassie a moment for her eyes to adjust to the darkness within the four walls. She could hear John walking further into the building.

After a while, the objects in front of her began to take shape. A table. A cabinet. The traces of hay on the hardwood floor.

Cassie furrowed her eyebrows in confusion. That was when John came back to her, nodding in understanding.

"I know what you must think, ma'am," he said. "Unfortunately, one of my pigs ran into the house a few days ago. I didn't have time to clean all of this up."

"You have... pigs?"

John kept his eyes on the floor, though the surprise in Cassie's tone made him glance up. "Yes, ma'am."

Her sense of smell began to catch up with her brain. Cassie didn't want to be rude, so she chose not to mention the stench.

"Could I have a glass of water, please?"

John cleared his throat and pointed to the front door. "Let me show you the well."

She waited for him to exit before following him back outside. Some part of her was relieved to be out in the sun again.

Luckily, the well wasn't too long of a walk. When John bent down to grab a bucket and tossed it down the endless pit, Cassie realized that there was a high probability that she would have to drink out of a trough.

"You'd have to get fresh water each morning," John said. "Normally, a full bucket will last me the whole day. You'd pour it into a pitcher, and then you'd pour it into a glass."

John pulled on the thick rope until the bucket appeared in his hands again. He placed it on the stone of the well before glancing over at Cassie. He looked her up and down.

"Don't worry about the bucket," he said. "I'll get it over to the kitchen each morning. You can do the rest."

Cassie didn't know whether she should have been offended or not. On one hand, he was being a gentleman. On the other, he was assuming that she wasn't capable of certain jobs before getting to know her.

She clasped her hands together in front of her. "I understand."

"Oh, I'm sorry... your water." John glanced back into the bucket. "I'll get you a glass from the kitchen. This way."

John lifted the bucket with one hand before walking past Cassie and towards the ranch house. She couldn't help but focus on his broad back as she followed. It looked like he had been a rancher since adolescence.

When they returned to the house, Cassie tried to ignore the mess around her. She couldn't even think about cleaning. All she wanted to do was have a seat and calm her nerves.

A surprisingly clean glass of water was thrust into her hand. The cold moisture around it coated her palm. Cassie closed her eyes as she took a small sip.

"Would you like to sit down?" she heard John's voice. "You look flushed, ma'am."

"Thank you," she choked out.

Cassie fell back, glad that there was a chair behind her. The heat was getting to her head. The smell of dung didn't help. Despite her feelings, she did not want to appear like a complete fool in front of John.

When Cassie felt a wave of nausea coming over her body, she suppressed it. And then she opened her eyes.

After taking another sip of water, she began to feel better.

John was crouching slightly in her peripheral vision. "You're not used to the heat. I get that."

Cassie stayed silent. She was set on reserving her energy for the tasks around the ranch. If John was as eager as he seemed, then he was due to give her a tour of the property shortly.

"Would you like to rest in the bedroom, ma'am?" he offered. "I'll leave you alone for a short while if you wish."

"That would be nice, thank you."

***

Cassie felt somewhat normal again around midday. Still, she was glad she didn't have to work outside. It made her feel sorry for John. Ranching was his whole life. It was no wonder he had such tanned skin.

Self-consciously, Cassie glanced down at her hands to see that they were almost as pale as snow.

"I can give you a tour, if you like," John broke the silence in the room.

Cassie gasped softly, a reaction which made John's lips twitch in amusement.

"I'm sorry, I didn't mean to scare you."

"No, it's fine," Cassie replied. "The tour... I can wait till the evening. Or maybe even tomorrow. I think I'm going to make a start in here first."

John glanced around the room as she gestured to the dirty floor. It was like he couldn't see the damage. He had probably gotten used to living in this state.

"Alright," John nodded. "You don't have to rush into the cleaning if you don't want to. It's your house too. I don't want you to feel like a hired hand."

A hired wife, more like.

Cassie shook the condescending voice out of her head. "No, I want to... I want to do something."

"Let me know if you need anything," John replied. "I'll be tending to the horses."

Cassie gave him a nod. "Okay, thank you."

Her eyes lingered on the front door after John had already walked away. She scratched her shoulder, narrowing her eyes at the flying insect by the porch. It was best to leave the door open since it was so stuffy inside.

Besides, she needed to sweep all of the hay out of the house anyway.

Cassie didn't hesitate. She grabbed a broom and got to work.

Strangely, the process of cleaning felt therapeutic. Obviously, she had involved herself in chores back at home, but never to this extent. The fact that she would be the only one cleaning for the rest of her life weighed heavily on her shoulders.

Would she ever find the time to write her poetry?

She didn't want to focus on her relationship with John just yet. It was already strange enough that she knew nothing about him. Cassie wanted to have the power to slow down time. She wanted to settle in. She wanted to get to know more people in town before it came to sharing a bed with a stranger. She wondered how a proper conversation between her and John would start. Would it come naturally at the dinner table? Would it have to be planned?

Cassie took a deep breath as she stopped sweeping and leaned against the broom. Her eyes scanned the wooden floorboards below her. Most of the hay was now on the porch and out of the house. The smell of dung had dwindled.

She propped the broom against the nearest wall. Her first instinct was to check behind her. She could see that John was digging through a pile of hay in the distance.

She was alone.

Cassie tried to convince herself there was nothing wrong with going wherever she wanted. After all, this was her house too.

But it still felt strange.

Cassie sighed as she took a step towards the doorframe. When she was close enough, it was evident that a door had never been installed. There were no holes in the wood, and no nails were sticking out.

Stepping through, Cassie found herself in a small space with three different doors around her. She had never been in any of those rooms before. However, her curiosity was getting the better of her.

Without thinking anything of it, she opened the closest door and peeked inside.

Cassie was underwhelmed to find a very dim storage room. Still, she made a note in her head to look through all of the cleaning supplies in there later.

After closing the first door, she moved over to the next one. The second room was slightly brighter as it had a large window. Cassie smiled somewhat as she walked forward, gazing out at the beautiful plains that looked like they stretched on for miles. Though the ranch was messy, she had to admit that it had been built on a gorgeous piece of land.

Cassie folded her arms over her chest, looking around the rest of the room. There was a single bed with an old dresser placed beside it. Perhaps it was a room for guests. It didn't look as if John liked to be in here. There was a thin layer of dust everywhere.

Just as Cassie was about to turn around and leave, a piece of paper on the wall caught her eye. John didn't strike her as the type of man to hang up sentimental items, which was why she found it odd to see one in front of her.

She narrowed her eyes and stepped closer.

It looked like a charcoal drawing. It wasn't very detailed or accurate. Clearly, it had been drawn by a child.

Cassie focused on the three stick figures on the paper. Aside from the main feature of the drawing, there were small scribbles in the background. Perhaps they resembled trees. It was difficult to tell.

The room was silent for a long while until Cassie heard the door creaking.

She jumped up, her eyes widening.

"What are you doing in here?" John asked rudely.

Cassie placed both hands on her chest as if to slow down her heart rate. Immediately, she felt embarrassed.

"Oh, I'm so sorry," she replied. "I just... I was just—"

"You shouldn't be snooping," John grumbled. "I didn't show you around yet."

"I'm sorry. I didn't mean to..."

John didn't stick around to hear the end of her sentence. Cassie felt her whole face burning in shame. Shortly after, she ran out of the room, shutting the door behind her.

Whatever trust John had before was most probably gone.

Chapter 3

Cassie had spent the first night at the ranch in just as much distress as she had during the day. First of all, she had slept in her husband's bed. Second of all, her husband was nowhere to be seen.

She had managed to stay awake for hours until her fatigue was finally strong enough to drag her under the blanket of sleep. When she woke up, John wasn't there.

A part of her was concerned. Another part was relieved.

If there had been some sort of accident on the ranch, she was no longer married. She was a free woman.

Cassie had to tug on her hair to rid herself of the foul thoughts. It wasn't right to think like that. She had been taught better.

The sun was a few inches above the horizon when Cassie got out of bed. She pulled her lightest dress over her head and fixed her brown hair into a bun. Regardless of what had happened, she felt more prepared today.

When she walked into the kitchen, the front door was open.

Cassie felt relief washing over her body when her eyes settled on John. He was leaning forward on the wooden banister on the porch, looking out at the fields.

Thinking of getting started on breakfast, Cassie moved over to the counter. As she searched the cupboards for food, her mind jumped back to what had happened last night. She recalled the child's drawing on the wall. She remembered the three stick figures.

Did John have a child? If so, why hadn't he introduced her to the kid?

Cassie was as clueless as she was yesterday, but she felt confident in the fact that John had been ignoring her ever since that incident.

She shouldn't have snooped. She knew better.

Cassie kept her attention on the task at hand when she heard John's footsteps behind her. She didn't want to make a fool out of herself again.

"Good morning," John said.

Cassie turned around to face him. "Good morning. How are you feeling?"

John seemed surprised by her question, yet he simply nodded and took a seat at the table. "I'm alright... did you sleep okay?"

"I did," Cassie lied. "Did you?"

"Yes," he said.

She got the feeling that he wasn't being honest either.

As curious as she was to know where John had been for the whole night, she decided to keep her mouth shut. She did not want to step over the line again.

Cassie turned back to the cupboards and continued to search for food. She was finally satisfied when she found some wrapped salted pork and a tin of beans. That should have made for a hearty breakfast.

Without looking back at her new husband, she began to cook. It didn't take long, but it felt like hours. Most of it was due to the silence. The only sound that Cassie could hear was the livestock outside and the clatter of kitchen utensils as she focused on the beans.

After dividing the food between two plates, Cassie placed one of them in front of John. He didn't waste any time in tucking in.

"Thank you," he said.

Cassie nodded and took a seat on the opposite side of the table.

They ate in silence until Cassie found the courage to speak up. Her heart was hammering against her chest before the words left her mouth.

"Where did you sleep during the night?"

John glanced up at her briefly. He swallowed his mouthful. "In the barn."

Cassie couldn't help but feel like she was the worst wife in the world. She was bad enough to scare her husband into sleeping with the animals. In a barn.

What was wrong with her?

She poked a single bean with her fork, keeping her eyes on the plate. She had to fight the urge to look upset. She didn't want to seem weak.

"One of the cows is pregnant," John said suddenly. "I didn't want to leave her side. She's getting close to her date."

Cassie stared up at him. "What?"

John raised an eyebrow as they locked gazes.

"I mean... your cow... I didn't know that she was pregnant," Cassie stammered.

"Well, how could you? I didn't tell you anything about the animals."

"I suppose," Cassie replied.

She found it hard to keep the relief out of her voice. At least she now knew that John didn't move into the barn because of her.

"It's my fault," John sighed. "I should have shown you around yesterday. But I was so busy with the ranch."

"No, you don't have to apologize," Cassie said.

"I'll show you after you've finished eating," he replied. "We will take a look while the sun still has mercy."

Cassie glanced towards the open door. At the same time, John placed his fork on top of the empty plate.

She wondered why John wasn't getting up from his seat. And then it dawned on her that he was waiting for her. Despite everything, he still had a firm hold on his manners.

***

Cassie saw dozens of cows and a large group of pigs within the ranch fence as she walked alongside John. He had a lot of animals, and the reason why she was here asserted itself again.

"That's the troublemaker that ran into the house a few days ago." John pointed at a spotty pig. "He's always eager to go somewhere."

Cassie smiled as they followed a path leading them towards the barn.

"You won't have to do any of the work out here," he added. "I don't expect a lady to be hauling bales of hay at four in the morning every day. But... it's good to get used to the surroundings, don't you think?"

"It's nice out here," Cassie replied. "If you ignore the smell."

John smiled as he kept his eyes on the ground. "Speaking of the smell... you did an outstanding job with the floor in the house. Thank you for that."

It felt odd to receive a compliment from a man as reserved as John, but Cassie took it gratefully. Even so, her mind was still lingering on the drawing. She was hoping that John would mention it first. Maybe all she had to do was to be patient. She had to remember that he wasn't prying at all.

When the couple got to the ranch's edge, Cassie grabbed the wooden fence and looked out into the plains. If a person were unlucky enough to get lost here, they'd have little chance of survival. The sun would do most of the work. The wild animals would finish them off.

Cassie had to squint against the sun to notice a little house in the distance.

"What's that?" she pointed.

John slid both hands into the pockets of his ranch pants as he followed her finger. "Ah, that's our neighbors."

"I didn't know we had neighbors." Cassie looked up at him.

"Well, they live so far away that they might as well be in a different state," John said. "You wouldn't walk there. You'd have to take a wagon, especially in this weather.

It's the farthest house from the town. Ours is second."

Cassie decided to ignore the strange feeling she got in the pit of her stomach when John referred to his house as *theirs*. Would she ever get used to the fact that she was now married?

"Do you talk to them?" Cassie nodded towards the house. "The ones that live there."

"Sometimes," John replied. "It's a small family. A couple and a child. Maybe you'll run into them soon."

Cassie nodded slowly before looking back at John's ranch. It would have been nice to get to know somebody in California. She didn't want to feel isolated.

"Shall we head back?" John took a step away from the fence. "I don't want you to pass out here."

Cassie grinned as she began to walk after her husband. "I feel better today. Thank you for asking."

She was left stunned when John chuckled at her words. It was the first time she had heard such a sound coming out of his mouth.

The walk back to the ranch house was pleasant. Their silence was comfortable, and Cassie didn't feel the need to make small talk. She guessed that John had a lot to think about too. It was easy to forget that he was in the same position as her.

He, too, had married a stranger.

"I want to post a letter to my mother," Cassie blurted out.

John stopped at the well, using the small roof to get his head into the shade. The bucket was gone. It looked like John kept his promise of fetching water in the mornings.

"Of course," he replied. "I can arrange for a wagon to pick you up."

"You're not going to come with me?"

Cassie began to regret her words as soon as they came out. She didn't want to sound desperate.

John smiled slightly. "Would you be okay on your own? I have work to do here, and the town is very safe."

"Yes," she nodded. "I don't mind." She realized she might enjoy a little time on her own, anyway.

"I'll give you some money too," he straightened up. "While you're there, it might be a good idea to get some food. We're running low... and I don't have much time to do these chores."

John scratched the back of his head sheepishly as he cast his gaze away from his wife.

"I'd like to do that," Cassie said. "Is there anything you need?"

"I'll write up a list," John replied.

Cassie glanced over to the ranch house. A part of her was excited to get out for a while. She rarely had moments to herself. It was like her whole life had been controlled by somebody else.

"I must get back to work," John cleared his throat. "I'll be around the barn today."

"Yes, I won't keep you," Cassie smiled. "I'll get started on dinner."

Instead of replying, John simply nodded before walking away. Cassie kept her eyes on him until he disappeared behind the barn. After that, she turned around and went into the house.

Chapter 4

After a few days on the ranch, Cassie finally began to feel herself settling in. John always kept himself away from the main house, using his pregnant cow as an excuse to do so. Cassie didn't know what to think. Either he didn't like her company, or he was genuinely passionate about his animals.

However, Cassie couldn't help but wonder if it was for the best. Maybe they needed some time apart from each other to grow closer together. Cassie was new to marriage, and she appreciated taking things slowly.

Cassie tucked a strand of hair behind her ear as the kitchen filled up with steam. She crouched in front of the fire and stirred the beef stew around in the pot. Cassie had managed to get a lot of provisions from town with the money that John had given her. As well as that, she had sent her first letter to her mother. She chose not to talk about her emotions in the letter. It was very matter-of-fact. But so was her mother.

Cassie glanced over to the front door when she heard heavy footsteps on the porch. Within a few seconds, John walked into the house, a small smile on his face.

She couldn't help but smile back. "Hi."

"Ma'am." John tipped his hat before taking it off and hanging it on the nail by the doorframe.

"How is it going out there?" she asked, turning back to face the stew. She didn't need to look at John to know that he had already taken his seat.

"One of the pigs is ready for slaughter," he said. "I was thinking that we could salt the meat. It should last for a while... have you ever done that before?"

Cassie shook her head. "No, I'm sorry."

"It's alright, I'll teach you," John replied. "We rely heavily on pork here. Plus, it sells for a lot."

Cassie grabbed two bowls and poured the stew into each one with a ladle.

"Do I have to watch you slaughtering a pig?" she asked, placing the bowl in front of him.

John grinned slightly. "No, I won't make you. Unless you really want to."

Cassie giggled softly as she took her seat on the opposite side of the table. She was comfortable with sharing her space with

John, but there were a few obstacles in her way that prevented her from opening up. She was confident that all of it would change with time, however.

They ate together in silence, listening to the birds chirping outside. It wasn't long until John had finished his meal and jumped up to his feet, ready to work again.

"Thank you, ma'am," he smiled, grabbing his hat off the nail. "I better get to it."

Cassie stood up and nodded at him.

When he was gone, the house fell silent yet again.

She knew that she wasn't lonely. That couldn't have been what she was feeling. Perhaps it was just that Cassie longed for another voice in the house.

Maybe she could meet up with John near the barn one day. Perhaps she could help him out with feeding the animals.

Cassie sighed as she grabbed the two bowls and placed them on the side. She didn't want to rush anything. She imagined that John would have been rather annoyed if she started to push her way into his workspace.

It just wasn't the time yet.

***

Cassie looked at the sky while keeping her hand on her hat. There wasn't a cloud in sight. It must have been challenging to maintain a ranch during the summer, especially when there was no promise of rainfall.

There was so much inspiration for poetry in the landscape. It was unfortunate that she barely had any time to write it all down.

Quickly, she snapped out of her thoughts.

Cassie focused on the clothesline swaying with the wind in front of her. She grabbed it before tossing a damp shirt over the rope. Even though the fabric had been outside for no longer than ten minutes, it was almost dry already.

All of a sudden, she heard the sound of approaching horse's hooves behind her. Knowing that John was busy with work in the barn, it spooked her. Who could it be? However, when Cassie turned around, she saw a blonde woman riding a gray mustang.

The horse had already crossed into the private land of the ranch, and it showed no signs of stopping.

Cassie abandoned the empty woven basket and started to walk towards the road where the horse was bound to end up.

Her heart was racing. She wasn't expecting company. Neither was John.

When the stranger pulled the horse's reins closer to her chest, the beast slowed down. It was good to know that she had no intentions of trampling Cassie.

"Hello," Cassie called out. "Can I help you?"

The woman looked confused, though she smiled down at Cassie. "Good afternoon."

Cassie waited until the woman hopped off the saddle. She landed on her feet, causing a small cloud of dust to jump off the ground. Her curiosity grew with each step that the stranger took in her direction.

"You must be new here," she smiled. "My name is Lilly Watson."

Cassie folded her arms over her chest. "Nice to meet you. My name is Cassie."

Lilly didn't seem too interested in what Cassie had to say. Instead, her gaze traveled over her shoulder as if she was looking for something. Or someone.

"Can I help you?" Cassie repeated.

"I don't suppose you've seen John, have you?" Lilly asked. "John Walker?"

"I've seen John," Cassie replied. "He is my husband."

Lilly snapped her eyes back to Cassie. She seemed genuinely shocked. "Your husband? When did he get married?"

"A few days ago," Cassie replied.

She didn't understand why she was being so blunt with a stranger. Perhaps it had something to do with the way the woman seemed a bit rudely disinterested in her.

Lilly reached up and brushed a few strands of hair out of her face. "Well... I guess me and him have a lot to catch up on," Lilly sighed. "Thank you for telling me."

"I'm sorry. Who are you?"

Lilly smiled in amusement. "Where are my manners? I should have told you earlier. I live by your ranch... in that little house near the hill."

Cassie watched as Lilly pointed toward the building that John had shown her. She was the neighbor? And she rode all the way out here on a horse just to speak to John? Alone?

Cassie took a deep breath to calm her nerves. She didn't like brazen people.

"Oh, yes," Cassie replied unenthusiastically. "John told me about a small family that lives in that house. You're married too?"

Lilly's smile faltered for a second. "I am. And I guess that it will be nice to have somebody else in the same position living so close by. We could trade items. And gossip!"

"That sounds wonderful... but not today," Cassie said. "I am quite busy with housework at the moment. And John is busy with the barn. I think that he wants to start salting some pork tomorrow."

Lilly nodded, her eyes lingering on the barn. "Well, it wasn't a wasted journey if I got to meet you."

"Would you like a glass of water before you leave?" Cassie offered, mustering her manners.

"No, I have a canteen on my horse," Lilly said. "Will you tell John that I was here? He'll probably visit me shortly. We have a lot to talk about."

"Of course," Cassie replied.

She didn't take her eyes off Lilly as she mounted her mare. It didn't sit well with her that Lilly found so much spare time that she could ride her horse to John's property.

Where was her husband? What about her child? Did she not have any responsibilities?

"I'll see you again at some point." Lilly grinned, turning her horse to face the ranch exit. "I hope you're settling in well."

Cassie opened her mouth to reply, but Lilly was too quick. She knocked her heels against her mare and trotted off into the distance, leaving a trail of dust behind her.

When Lilly was nothing but a speck on the plains, Cassie turned to look at the barn. The double doors were open, but John was nowhere to be seen.

Would he have stepped out to greet Lilly if he'd seen her?

Chapter 5

The first cloudy day on the ranch was accompanied by a gentle breeze and distant sounds of thunder. But of course, work for John didn't stop, which meant that she was alone.

Cassie took a deep breath of fresh air as she settled on a wooden bench by the shade of the ranch house. Her journal fell open in her lap, guiding her to the next blank page.

She had to be careful with taking this time for herself. However, she was certain that most of the household tasks had already been completed. Dinner had been prepared, the floors had been swept, and the whole house was dusted. The only job left was to collect the dry clothes off the washing line.

But she had some time to herself now. It was rare, and Cassie began to write.

The words came naturally. She didn't have to think. She wanted to note her experience with meeting John and coming to the ranch.

Cassie didn't realize that she had started to echo the words she had sent to her mother.

A stranger, but my husband.

In the land of unforgiving weather.

She closed her eyes when her thoughts traveled over to Lilly.

A poem about Lilly. Well, that had to be a completely different text entirely.

Cassie knew she didn't like her, but she didn't know why. And knowing that she was going to live so close to her for the rest of her life was unnerving. She wanted to know about Lilly's history with John. Were they friends? Was there something going on that Cassie knew nothing about?

She dropped her pencil into the middle of her journal and leaned back on the bench. Cassie knew that she was lucky. She had a husband who was kind to her. He worked hard and seemed clever and generous. It could have been so much worse, and she felt like she needed to mature in her thinking. Nothing was as bad as it seemed.

Cassie was about to pick up her pencil again when she heard a horse's loud whinny.

She lifted her eyes from her journal, spotting a galloping horse in one of the corrals. John was in the saddle.

Cassie felt her breath hitching as the young mare began to kick out her hind legs.

The animal was trying to buck him off. It was frightening to watch, but John seemed to be content with what he was doing.

He even had a trace of a smile on his lips.

Cassie got off the bench and rushed over to the corral, grabbing the fence with both hands. Her instincts told her to scream at him to get his attention, but she didn't want to spook the horse. She didn't want to be the cause of an accident.

John allowed the mare to kick up a fuss in the corral. A few minutes later, it began to gallop, following the fence all the way around. When the mare got close enough to Cassie, John slowed her down.

He furrowed his eyebrows, patting his horse's neck.

"Cassie," he seemed out of breath. "I didn't know that you were watching."

She smiled slightly, gesturing to the bench. "I was taking a break. Are you okay?"

"I'm fine," he grinned. "Just trying to tame this mare. She's the newest horse on the ranch. A lot of energy. Maybe one day she will simmer down enough for you to ride her."

"Oh, I don't know about that," Cassie giggled.

John wrapped the reins around one of his wrists as he attempted to keep the horse still. "I need to wear her out. Forgive me."

"No, go ahead," Cassie stepped back, smiling as John kicked his heels against the horse and sent her into a gallop again.

Two laps later, the dust was flying around the corral. But the mare was no longer skittish and seemed eager to continue. She was rearing to go as she grew more comfortable with having John in the saddle.

John leaned down to pat her neck again before doing another lap. When he came back to where Cassie was waiting, he wiped the sweat off his forehead.

"Wanna have a go?"

Cassie had to laugh. "You want me to tame a horse?"

"You don't have to tame one," John replied. "But it'd be good for you to introduce yourself to another mare. I want you to have a horse that you trust... and vice versa."

"I don't know the first thing when it comes to riding horses."

John tilted his head to the side. "You don't?"

"No, I'd probably fall off," Cassie grinned. "A lot."

"Well, now I want to teach you even more," John smiled. "Come on, it's the perfect weather for riding."

Cassie played with her fingers nervously, glancing over to the barn. She didn't want to embarrass herself in front of John. But, on the other hand, it could be an opportunity to grow closer.

"Do you have riding pants?" John glanced down at her dress.

"Actually, I do," Cassie replied. "I'll be back in a moment... I should get changed."

John tipped his hat her way. "I'll be right here, ma'am."

Cassie turned to the bench and rushed over to her journal, picking it up and tucking it under her arm. After that, there was nothing left to do but make her way into the house. Even though she was a bit afraid of riding a horse, she was also somewhat excited.

Her smile lingered as she changed into a pair of beige pants and a light shirt. She felt grateful that her mother insisted on making her pack a pair of pants. Though she'd had no use for them back in North Carolina, she'd known things were bound to change in the west.

When she came out of the house, she saw that John was standing next to his young horse within the corral. His mouth was moving. She wasn't close enough to hear what was being said.

Cassie cleared her throat as she approached her husband. "Do I get to pick the horse?"

John turned to look at her as he smiled. "I have an older mare in the stables. She'll go easy on you." He chuckled before gesturing to the barn with his head. "Come on, I'll show you."

Cassie walked on the outside of the corral, letting her fingers linger on the wooden fence to her left. John was walking beside her, though the fence separated them.

"What's her name?" Cassie asked, glancing over at the tan horse.

"Maggie," John replied, a proud look on his face. "Named her after my great-grandmother. She had the same spirit."

Cassie bit her bottom lip. It was the most information about John's personal life he had ever shared. She decided not to question him any further. She didn't want him to close himself off again.

"Can you hold the reins?" John asked when they got to the barn. "You don't have to go over to this side. Just make sure that she doesn't scamper away."

"Okay." Cassie reached out to grab the reins as John hopped over the fence and jogged into the barn.

Cassie tried not to make eye contact with the mare in fear that she would start to kick up a fuss. Instead, Cassie hung the top half of her body over the fence, keeping her fingers wrapped around the leather straps. It seemed that Maggie was just as awkward as

Cassie. She was keeping her head perfectly still.

After a few minutes, John emerged from the barn, leading a larger horse behind him. He grinned widely when his eyes fell on Cassie.

"You alright there?"

"I don't want to spook her," Cassie replied.

John stepped closer and took the reins from her hand. "Here. Let's swap."

Cassie breathed a sigh of relief as they exchanged the reins.

"This is Ruby," John said, patting the black horse on the head. "I know that she's much larger than Maggie, but she's slow. And she doesn't buck."

"Let's not speak too soon," Cassie grinned. "I might be the exception."

John laughed softly. It sounded like a warm fire on a cold winter's day. It was enough to put her nerves at ease.

"How do I pull myself up?"

John tied Maggie's reins to the fence quickly. "Oh, here. Allow me."

Cassie felt the air leaving her lungs when John grabbed her around the waist and hoisted her up. She gasped when she landed on the saddle. She didn't know how to react.

"Just put your right leg over and onto the other side," John pointed.

All Cassie could do was nod. She followed his instructions silently before grabbing the reins with both hands. To her relief, Ruby didn't seem to have realized that there was a person on her back. However, at that point, Cassie would have preferred to have been bucked off. She knew that her face was as red as a tomato.

John rushed over to the entrance of the corral and opened the gate. "Through here. Tap with your heels gently and she will move forward."

Cassie felt several emotions at once, and being afraid of falling was now top on the list. Somehow, she managed to walk Ruby into the corral where John was waiting for her. He mounted his mare within a second, making it look like it required no effort. He must have been very experienced with horses.

"It's not too bad, is it?" he grinned, lining Maggie up with Ruby. "Do you feel okay?"

Cassie nodded quickly. "Yes. I-I'm fine."

The next time Cassie glanced over her shoulder was when they reached the other end of the corral. She smiled slightly, feeling proud for maintaining control of her horse. She knew it was probably nothing special, but it was her first time, and she did it.

Maggie whinnied quietly as John patted her neck again. "She's very eager, this one. But I think that she will settle just fine over time. I bought her for no more than six dollars. Wild ones aren't very expensive as they are hard to train."

"And you're certain that you'll tame her?"

John gave Cassie a small grin. "That's one of my jobs on the ranch, ma'am."

When the couple completed their first lap together, John straightened his back.

"Ready to go faster?"

"Faster?" Cassie widened her eyes. "Are you sure that I'll be able to control her?"

"You do not have to worry about Ruby, ma'am," John said. "She's a gentle horse. Besides, she is contained in the corral. It's not like she'll just gallop away."

"What if she jumps over the fence?"

John laughed. "Her jumping days are over. You will be okay."

Cassie smiled as her confidence grew. Maybe she could get used to this.

"Alright, let's do it," Cassie replied. "Do I tap my heels again?"

"That's correct."

"What if I want to slow down?"

"Well, in that case, you will have to pull on the reins gently. Give it a go."

Cassie took a deep breath before sending Ruby into a trot. John stayed behind her as she took off. She could hear him laughing.

"You're a natural!"

Cassie tried to suppress her smile, but it was too big for her face. She enjoyed how the breeze made its way through her hair, letting some parts of it fall loose. It was a pleasant contrast to the heat.

As time went on, Cassie began to feel more relaxed. She didn't have to clench the reins too tightly. She started to trust Ruby. It was a pleasure to trot around the corral, knowing that she was in safe hands.

Cassie glanced over at John just in time to see him galloping past her. He made everything look so easy. And the smile on his face made him look like he didn't have a care in the world.

"Slow down, Ruby," Cassie said, pulling on the reins gently. "Let's slow down."

Satisfied that Ruby had listened to her rider, Cassie reached down to pat her neck. She knew she would remember this feeling for a long time. Riding a horse felt like freedom. She wanted to put it into words. She had to write a poem later.

"Have you had enough?" John called out from the other side of the corral.

Cassie smiled at him. "I think that Ruby needs some rest. Like you said, she's quite old."

"Come around to the fence," John replied. "I'll help you off the saddle."

***

Cassie could feel her heart racing in her chest. Her thighs were aching from straddling a horse, but she couldn't stop smiling.

Why hadn't she done this sooner?

A part of her was excited that she could start riding any time she wanted. She lived on this ranch now. It belonged to her as much as it belonged to John.

"Here," John said.

When Cassie looked up at him, he was holding a glass of water. "Oh, thank you."

John sat down next to her before sipping from his own glass. It seemed that he was ready to have a break. Cassie felt delighted that he had chosen to spend this time with her.

"A few more lessons and you'll be ready to ride into town," John said.

Cassie turned her head in his direction, keeping her eyes on his hands. She felt like making eye contact with him would have made her blush. For some reason, she had started to see him in a different light.

"Have you always had horses on your ranch?" she asked.

John was careful with his reply. "No, I got my first wild one a year ago. I wanted to be able to train it until it was fit enough for the ordinary folk. Nobody likes an unpredictable horse."

"So, you're an entrepreneur," Cassie grinned.

John chuckled softly. "I ain't nothing but a rancher."

Cassie bit the inside of her cheek at her impulse to ask more questions. She was very curious about the man next to her.

He was kind-hearted and smart... but was there another side to him?

"Can I ask you a question?" John blurted out.

Cassie swallowed hard before nodding.

"What did you do back in North Carolina?" John looked at her. "I corresponded with your mother very briefly. Unfortunately, she didn't give me a lot of details."

Cassie had to wipe her sweaty palms against her knees. She didn't know why she suddenly felt like she had to impress him.

"I wrote poetry," she said. "I still do... when I get the chance."

John smiled warmly as he leaned back against the bench. "Is that why I saw you walking around with a journal?"

"Yes, that would explain it," Cassie giggled.

She felt her whole body relaxing at John's reaction. Some men didn't like the fact that a woman might have been smarter than them, but John was different.

"Can I see some of it?" he asked.

When Cassie took a deep breath, he raised both hands as if he were about to surrender.

"Oh, but you don't have to show me now," he added. "Whenever you feel like it... and only if you want to."

Cassie had to laugh. "I'd love to show you at some point. But I think that I left my journal in the bedroom."

"Did you sell your poetry in North Carolina?"

"Sometimes," she replied, glancing back at her glass of water. "Rarely. I hope to pursue it here in California."

"Yes, it's always good to occupy yourself with something other than work," John said. "I just want you to know that I won't stand in your way. I don't own you, Cassie. Despite what all of this might feel like."

Cassie looked up at him to see that his eyes had softened. "Thank you. That means a lot."

John didn't reply. He simply stared into her eyes.

After a while, it became very difficult to look away. Cassie took a sip of water and swallowed hard as her face flushed. She became very aware of the fact that their legs were close to touching.

Cassie cleared her throat, forcing herself to break eye contact. She needed to change the subject. She needed to say something. Anything!

"Somebody called Lilly came to the ranch," she blurted out.

John raised both eyebrows in surprise. "Oh... when was this?"

"You were busy in the barn," she explained. "I didn't want to distract you."

John reached up and scratched at the stubbly patch near his jawline. His eyebrows knitted together.

"She wanted to talk to you about something," Cassie shrugged one shoulder. "She also said that she lives in that little house by the hill."

John smiled slightly before nodding. "Yes, she does."

"Forgive me, but I thought you hinted that you weren't very close to that family."

"I'm not," John's smile widened. Perhaps he enjoyed seeing Cassie suffer. Anybody from a mile away could tell that she didn't want to pry, yet she couldn't help herself.

Cassie pinched the material of her pants as she kept her eyes down. "You're not?"

"Maybe I should explain the situation," John chuckled, looking back at the horizon. "I have known her family for a very long time... our children used to play together. My wife would always ride over to their house, and they'd trade their bread for our pork. We always had good relations."

When John glanced over at Cassie, he noticed that her mouth was ajar.

"I should have told you this before," he sighed.

Cassie bit the inside of her cheek as realization began to creep onto her face. John used to be married. She didn't know that.

Did that change anything? No. But it was somewhat of a shock.

"My wife died recently," John continued. "It was tuberculosis... shortly after her death, my daughter got infected too. She suffered the same fate."

Cassie placed a hand on her chest. "I'm so sorry."

"Ain't your fault, ma'am," John replied. "I guess that their deaths changed everything, though. I couldn't find the time to work on the ranch, and when I did, I couldn't bring myself to work. Most of my money went towards their funeral. Lilly and her family... they distanced themselves. But I'm sure that it was my fault too. I shut myself off."

Cassie closed her eyes as she listened to John's story. She didn't expect it to be so heartbreaking.

Why did she judge him so soon?

"I didn't know what to do," he muttered. "I was lost for a long time...I thought that I was going to lose the ranch. I had no money... well, I still have no money. But that's why you're here. I need your help... and I hope that you can forgive me for dragging you into this. I know that this is not the life you have imagined."

Cassie glanced over at him to see an expression of deep sorrow.

"I do not control you, Cassie," he said. "That's why I want you to pursue your dreams with poetry. It's the least I can do after everything that happened."

Cassie furrowed her eyebrows slightly. "My mother failed to mention that you had no money. I'm surprised that she chose you as my husband."

John smiled in her direction. "I may have misled her... but don't get me wrong. We will have money. I want to get the ranch up and running again. Within a few months, we should have a lot of customers buying our pork and beef. It just... it takes time."

Hesitantly, Cassie reached over and placed her hand on John's arm. He looked at her.

"I can't imagine the pain that you live with, John," she said. "And I know I won't be able to replace your late wife... but I will try my best to make you happy."

John smiled sadly and covered her hand with his. "As will I."

Chapter 6

As time went on, Cassie began to grow confident about her place on the ranch. It took her a while to get there, but she finally understood that John valued her. Not because he needed money, but because there was mutual respect.

She smiled widely as she walked into the kitchen with her mother's letter in her hand. She was content with her place in the world. It was true that being married to a stranger was still far from ideal, but she was learning to live with it. Besides, John was extremely pleasant. Cassie found herself yearning for the opportunity to be in his presence.

She wasn't sure if that had anything to do with her knowledge about his past. Cassie could see the deeply troubled man... and for some reason, he became more desirable.

She wiped the moisture off her forehead with a damp cloth before sitting at the kitchen table. Cassie had just returned from her time in town. She had purchased some food for the week, finding the time to visit the post office as well.

She was eager to read her mother's letter. She was hoping for some details about life in North Carolina. There was a small part of Cassie that missed her place of birth dearly.

She ripped the top of the envelope and pulled out the letter, a small smile lingering on her face.

However, as her eyes scanned through Ann's handwritten text, her smile began to fade.

It was easy to forget the troubles that she had left behind.

"My apologies," John's voice sounded in the room. "I didn't mean to distract you."

Cassie glanced up at her husband, noticing that he had a large burlap sack thrown over his shoulder. It looked heavy.

"That's okay; I'm not busy," she replied.

John walked into the house, pointing to the letter in her hand. "Your mother?"

Cassie smiled. "Yes, she wrote me back."

At first, Cassie didn't want to burden John with the details of the letter. But then she remembered that he was her husband and had every right to know.

"She said that money is running low," Cassie sighed. "I don't want it to get to a point where she has to move someplace else."

John frowned before dropping the bag near the table. It sounded like potatoes.

"We won't let it get to that point, ma'am," he said. "We will have more money at the end of the month. I just need to sell some of the cows and the horses. It takes time."

Cassie nodded slowly. "I know it does. We can't do much about it."

A part of her felt it was unfair that she had to worry about her mother. She had her own life now. She should have been free to live it in peace. But her past was always catching up to her.

Cassie read the letter again while John moved the potatoes into the nearest cupboard.

"Is there anything I can do to help with the ranch?" Cassie asked before placing the letter on the table.

She turned to look at John, who was grinning at her. "You're already doing more than enough, ma'am."

"Come on, there must be more I can do," Cassie replied. "And don't call me ma'am. It makes me feel old."

John chuckled as he leaned against the counter. "Alright, Cassie."

She smiled widely. Her name sounded good coming from his mouth.

"I guess that feeding the animals could be doable for you," he shrugged. "While you're doing that, I could find the time to look through the ledger. Sort out the cattle that I intend on selling. Maybe even ride into town to find a buyer."

"Yes." Cassie was excited as she got to her feet. "That sounds perfect. That will make the whole process faster."

"I must say that I appreciate your eagerness," John smiled. "I know that it's driven by the desire to help your mother, but I can tell that some part of you is showing genuine interest."

"Well, yes, it's my ranch too," Cassie grinned. "Of course I care what happens to it."

John glanced down at his feet as he folded his arms. Cassie knew that there was more that he wanted to say, but he refrained from doing so. Perhaps it wasn't the time yet.

***

It took Cassie a week to get into the swing of things.

John was right when he told her that managing a ranch was a lot of work. But Cassie was determined to get John's business up and running again.

In the mornings, she began to get up before the sun. Feeding the animals was the easiest part, but it took a lot of time. It was a big ranch.

While Cassie was taking care of the cattle, John was riding out into town. It became a routine. He was always hesitant about leaving her alone, but Cassie insisted that he needed to sell his cattle. The sooner he found a buyer, the sooner their money troubles would become a thing of the past.

One day, Cassie was tossing handfuls of seeds to the hens behind the barn. Her mind was racing. She had many ideas for the ranch. It was the first time she had been so invested in something.

She watched as the hens raced around their enclosure, pecking the seeds off the ground.

Her heart began to beat faster when she heard the sound of a galloping horse. John must be back from town.

Cassie locked the gate behind her before placing her basket of chicken feed on a wooden crate by the coop. She rushed over to the entrance of the barn, expecting to find John hitching his horse.

However, when she was close enough, she heard the sound of a woman's voice. Her instincts told her to hide, so she darted behind the barn door.

"It's like you've been avoiding me," Lilly's voice muttered nearby.

Cassie put a hand over her mouth to silence her breathing. What was she doing here?

"It's not avoidance," John replied. "I've been busy."

"You're always busy lately," she replied.

Cassie heard John's fake laugh. "I'm running a ranch. I have a wife. It's not personal."

Lilly took a long time to reply. "I've been lonely, John."

It took all Cassie's strength not to burst out from behind the doors and scream at the woman. Lilly's arrogance was setting her teeth on edge. It had the power to devalue Cassie's existence.

She was married to John. Yet, that didn't stop Lilly from going after him.

Was Cassie nothing but a ghost?

"What about your sisters?" John offered. "Your husband?"

So, she was married.

"It's complicated," Lilly replied, her voice sad. "They have their own lives. I'm not that important to them."

Suddenly, Cassie started to feel better about herself. Lilly was a beautiful woman who had the time to ride around California by herself. But clearly, that didn't make her happy.

Cassie sighed softly as she leaned against the wall and glanced around the barn. She shouldn't have been eavesdropping. But she couldn't help herself. It was a conversation that concerned her, after all. John was her husband.

And she had to admit that there was a spark of jealously inside of her.

"Why didn't you tell me that you were getting married?" Lilly asked, changing the subject altogether. "I had to hear it from some random woman that I've never even met."

John didn't hesitate with his response. "That random woman is my wife. And I'd ask that you show her some respect. Especially when you are on my land."

Cassie felt her cheeks flushing.

"I know that you're lonely," John continued. "But I'm not going to destroy my marriage for that."

"Why?" Lilly snapped back. "Do you love her?"

"Yes, I do."

Cassie felt like she couldn't breathe.

She shouldn't have been listening in to their conversation. At first, she was afraid that she was going to hear some sort of incriminating evidence. But she was wrong.

Cassie placed a hand to her chest as her heart started beating faster.

She didn't know what to do. But she knew that she didn't want to continue listening. She trusted John. He was a good man. And he was on her side.

Before Cassie could step away, she heard Lilly releasing a hollow laugh.

"That's not possible. You just met her! And you've known me for years!"

Cassie could tell that John was shaking his head. "I have nothing else to say to you."

"You're making a mistake, John."

Lilly huffed loudly before there was the sound of a horse whinnying. After that, the sound of horse hooves.

She was leaving.

Cassie should have done the same.

Without looking behind her, Cassie stepped backward. She could hear footsteps. John was getting closer.

She didn't want him to see her in here. She didn't want him to find out that she was eavesdropping.

Cassie panicked and picked up the pace. But before she could break into a jog, she stepped into an empty bucket. She gasped as she lost her balance and was a loud clatter.

In a split second, Cassie found herself falling to the floor. Before she could even hit the ground, everything went black.

Chapter 7

"Cassie?"

John's distant voice called to her.

"Cassie," he repeated. "Can you hear me?"

Her eyes fluttered open gently.

There was a dark haze around her vision, but in the middle of it was John. He had taken off his hat and started to fan her with it. That was when Cassie realized that she was still on the floor. John's strong arm was wrapped around her.

"You're okay," he said, a small smile finding his face. "You'll be okay."

Cassie felt a slight pulsing pain in her right leg. She tried to move it, wincing when the pain flared up.

"Try not to move," John said, glancing down to her feet. "I think that you've twisted your ankle."

"Oh, no," she whimpered.

"It's my fault," John sighed. "I knew that I shouldn't have left your side."

Cassie grinned slightly. "No, I'm a grown woman. And I chose to stay here on my own."

John placed his hat back on his head before pressing his free hand against her cheek. Cassie stared up at him.

"I think that the heat got to your head," John said. "What were you doing out here?"

"I was feeding the chickens," Cassie replied. "And then I... I tripped."

John nodded slowly. There was a mischievous flicker in his eyes. It was obvious that he knew more than he let on, but he chose to go along with Cassie's narrative.

"It was my fault," Cassie added quickly. "I just... I wasn't looking where I was going. That's what I get for being clumsy."

John smiled. She couldn't help the butterflies that took flight in the pits of her stomach.

"I found a seller for the cows," John said.

Cassie widened her eyes in excitement. "You did? That's great news!"

"Yeah, we'll use the money to fix your leg," he joked.

Cassie felt comfortable enough to gently slap his chest. She felt the shake of his laughter spreading throughout her body. The feeling reminded her that they were closer than they'd ever been. She was lying in his arms, and he was cradling her.

It all felt strangely familiar.

"I meant what I said, Cassie," John uttered.

Cassie tried to look confused, but she knew exactly what he was talking about. "About what?"

"About me loving you," he replied, his voice growing quieter. "I know that you heard me. It wasn't like I was whispering. The whole ranch heard me."

Cassie blushed as she broke eye contact.

She hadn't experienced a feeling like this before. She couldn't find the words for it.

John smiled warmly as he tucked a strand of hair behind her ear. "Please don't worry yourself about Lilly. She's got her own issues to deal with... and she doesn't have a good way of concealing them."

Cassie lowered her head to the side, leaning on John's chest.

"Whatever she says is irrelevant," John continued. "I know how I feel about you, and nobody is capable of changing my mind."

His eyes were the richest brown she'd ever seen. Cassie did all that she could to prevent herself from reaching out and touching his face.

"I feel the same," she replied, her voice barely above a whisper.

For a second, she wasn't even sure that John had heard her. But when his smile widened, she knew.

***

Cassie glanced up at the sky as thunder rumbled above her. It was deafening. She figured that the weather in California went from one extreme to the other, but she had learned how to live with it.

She had John by her side. Nothing scared her anymore.

It was late in the evening when the clouds pulled together, threatening to drop sheets of rain on the ranch. Cassie had a long walk back to the house. After taking it easy for a few days with her ankle, she knew that she could not rest any longer. Nobody could keep her still. She wanted the ranch to thrive.

Cassie sighed deeply as she glanced toward the house. It was a ten-minute walk from where she was standing. Her arm was aching from carrying a basket full of apples, but she felt a smile stretching over her face. Cassie hugged the basket with one arm after throwing the handle over her shoulder. Then, she began to walk back to the house.

A few minutes into her short journey, she heard the sound of a woman crying. It puzzled her. For a second, Cassie was convinced that the wind was playing tricks on her. However, when she passed a little shed by the fence, she spotted the familiar glint of blonde hair.

It was Lilly.

Cassie placed the basket on the ground and walked up to her neighbor. What was she doing here alone?

"Lilly?" Cassie called out gently.

Lilly wiped at her face desperately before standing up from her crouched position. She faked a smile.

"Are you okay?" Cassie asked.

"I'm fine," Lilly replied, glancing at her horse. The gray mare was grazing on a patch of grass a few feet away from the fence.

Cassie raised both eyebrows. She didn't like the woman, but it was troubling to see Lilly in that state.

"Ah, there's no point in lying to you," Lilly tipped her head back in expiration. "I'm not fine. In fact, I'm having a terrible day."

"Well, what's wrong?"

Cassie decided to forget about the fact that Lilly tried to court her husband a few days ago. She wasn't the kind of person to hold a grudge.

Before Lilly could reply, fresh tears started to fall down her face. "My husband is never home. My son, Toby, is always spending time with his aunt. I think he likes her more than me. I'm so… lonely."

"What about your friends?"

Lilly's lip began to tremble. "I'm ashamed to say I have no close friends."

Cassie looked up as the thunder rumbled above her head again. She was never good with advice, especially when it came to handing it out to people that weren't particularly pleasant to her. She struggled to find the words as she glanced back over to the ranch house uncomfortably.

"I shouldn't be telling you this," Lilly shook her head, wiping her wet cheeks. "It's... it's embarrassing. And you don't care, so..."

Cassie sighed. "Would you like me to walk you home?"

Lilly appeared to settle down, though when she was close to catching her breath, the sobbing took over her body again.

Cassie played with her fingers before taking a step forward.

"Please, don't do this," Cassie said. "I know you're in pain... but crying isn't going to solve anything."

"What will solve it then, Cassie?" Lilly asked. "I ain't an evil person, you know. But people treat me as though I am. I don't know if all of this would be happening if my husband was home more often. If I just knew that he loved me…"

Cassie folded her arms over her chest. "Have you talked to your husband about this?"

Lilly took a deep breath, her shoulders rising. "No. It would be a waste of time."

"I know that it can be hard to express your feelings," Cassie stepped forward, feeling more confident in her advice. "Would you... want me to help you?"

Lilly glanced from side to side as the first drop of rain hit the ground. The second one landed on Cassie's cheek.

"How would you help me?"

Cassie felt sad for the woman in front of her. Lilly had a roof over her head. She was lucky enough to have borne a child. She was married. Yet, a large part of her life was still missing.

They were vastly different, but Cassie and Lilly were both survivors of a cruel world. That similarity bonded them together. And if there was one thing that Cassie knew, it was the fact that being able to write held more power than feeble words.

"Can you read?" Cassie asked.

Lilly tilted her head to the side in confusion. "A little, why?"

Epilogue

Two years later...

The sky had been painted with a wonderful shade of blue when Cassie walked out of the house. She smiled and reached forward to grab the wooden banister of the porch.

Everything looked perfect.

"You ain't gonna keep it up like that," her husband's voice boomed in the distance. "You gotta nail it down!"

Cassie didn't have any trouble finding him. When her eyes settled on John, her smile grew wider.

He had his hands on his hips as he approached their newest ranch hand. The boy was called Billy. He had been hired to fix some of the fences around the property, but it was clear that he wasn't capable of holding a hammer.

Cassie couldn't help but giggle as she watched John pointing to the broken fence. "Grab the wood with one hand and then swing. Otherwise, you ain't going to hit the nail from that angle."

"Yes, sir," Billy nodded. "I understand. I'm sorry."

"That's okay," John grinned. "Just keep at it. You'll get the hang of it soon enough."

Cassie raised her hand to wave at her husband when he turned to face the house. He waved back enthusiastically, a massive grin on his face.

When the ranch business started to take off, the couple had no choice but to hire a few ranch hands. There were more cattle to herd.

There were more horses to tame. More fences to fix. And Cassie loved every minute of it.

Moreover, good business meant she could finally send her mother the money she needed to keep her house. Cassie felt fulfilled with her life. She was doing something that benefitted a lot of people. She wouldn't have had it any other way.

She gasped softly when she felt a small hand tugging on the back of her dress. She turned around, her gaze landing on the small boy behind her. Her son.

"There you are," Cassie said, crouching down to his level. "Did Lilly let you try those peaches?"

Tommy was a carbon copy of his father. The little boy nodded, wiping the peach juice off his chin with his hand. Cassie laughed.

"Delicious, aren't they?" she grinned.

Suddenly, a clatter came from inside the house. A few seconds later, Lilly appeared in the doorway. She looked panicked, but when her eyes found Tommy, she sighed in relief.

"That boy is a runner," she pointed at him.

Cassie giggled, lifting her son into her arms. "He is a runner. Almost as fast as Toby."

Lilly rolled her eyes playfully at the mention of her own son. "I don't even know where Toby is. He was helping me with the latest poem, but then he disappeared into the barn. I think he wants to help the others with the chickens."

"That would explain a lot," Cassie agreed.

She couldn't help but smile at Lilly. She brought a lot of energy to the ranch. When Cassie first met her, she had been convinced that Lilly would be her enemy. But she couldn't have been more wrong.

When Cassie taught Lilly how to read and write, it was as if her life began to fall into place. There was something so satisfying about the fact that she could teach Lilly about poetry. Over the years, it became a common interest. And now, they were creating poems together.

Also, the confidence had helped Lilly talk to her husband, and now she was helping him with his own business. They had more time together and were both happier.

"I better go and find him," Lilly sighed, gesturing over her shoulder. "I wrote a few lines. Let me know what you think when you get the chance. I think I should be heading home soon... same time tomorrow?"

Cassie smiled and nodded. "Of course. Looking forward to it."

Lilly returned her smile.

She poked at Tommy's cheek with one finger when she passed Cassie, skipping down the steps of the porch.

"See you soon, troublemaker," she said.

Tommy giggled, lifting one hand up to wave at her.

The air smelled fresh as the lilac flowers began to bloom around the property. The ranch was bursting with colors.

Sometimes, Cassie couldn't believe that she was this lucky.

She took a deep breath as her eyes returned to her husband. John was walking towards her, a mischievous grin on his face.

As he got closer, Tommy burst out in giggles.

"Somebody's been eating the peaches again," John said, joining Cassie on the porch.

Tommy laughed harder and harder until John grabbed the toddler out of his mother's arms and tossed him into the air. When he caught him again, Tommy shrieked with glee.

"When did I get so lucky?" John asked, looking down at his wife.

Cassie leaned up to kiss his cheek. "You know, I was just thinking the exact same thing."

The End

FREE GIFT

Just to say thanks for checking our works we like to gift you

Our Exclusive Never Before Released Books

100% FREE!

Please GO TO

http://cleanromancepublishing.com/gift

And get your FREE gift

Thanks for being such a wonderful client.

Please Check out My Other Works

By checking out the link below

http://cleanromancepublishing.com/fjauth

Thank You

Many thanks for taking the time to buy and read through this book.

It means lots to be supported by SPECIAL readers like YOU.

Hope you enjoyed the book; please support my writing by leaving an honest review to assist other readers.

.

With Regards,

Faith Johnson

Printed in Great Britain
by Amazon

32127199R00078